A NOTE TO PARENTS

When your children are ready to "step into reading," giving them the right books—and lots of them—is as crucial as giving them the right food to eat. **Step into Reading Books** present exciting stories and information reinforced with lively, colorful illustrations that make learning to read fun, satisfying, and worthwhile. They are priced so that acquiring an entire library of them is affordable. And they are beginning readers with an important difference— they're written on four levels.

Step 1 Books, with their very large type and extremely simple vocabulary, have been created for the very youngest readers. **Step 2 Books** are both longer and slightly more difficult. **Step 3 Books,** written to mid-second-grade reading levels, are for the child who has acquired even greater reading skills. **Step 4 Books** offer exciting nonfiction for the increasingly proficient reader.

Children develop at different ages. **Step into Reading Books,** with their four levels of reading, are designed to help children become good—and interested—readers *faster*. The grade levels assigned to the four steps—preschool through grade 1 for Step 1, grades 1 through 3 for Step 2, grades 2 and 3 for Step 3, and grades 2 through 4 for Step 4—are intended only as guides. Some children move through all four steps very rapidly; others climb the steps over a period of several years. These books will help your child "step into reading" in style!

For Pat Cummings, Kelly, and Mom

Library of Congress Cataloging-in-Publication Data
Milgrim, David. Why Benny barks / by David Milgrim. p.   cm. — (Step into reading. A Step 1 book)
SUMMARY: A child describes the possible reasons why Benny the dog barks.
ISBN 0-679-86157-2 (trade) — ISBN 0-679-96157-7 (lib. bdg.) [1. Dogs—Fiction.   2. Barking—Fiction.
3. Stories in rhyme.]   I. Title.   II. Series: Step into reading. Step 1 book.
PZ8.3.M5776Wh 1994 [E]—dc20   93-47102

Manufactured in Mexico   10 9 8 7 6 5 4 3

STEP INTO READING is a trademark of Random House, Inc.

Step into Reading™

Why Benny Barks

by
David
Milgrim

A Step 1 Book

Random House 🏠 New York

There are many things
that I'll never know.

But why Benny barks
does puzzle me so.

He barks when we're out.

He barks when we're home.

Benny stands by himself
and barks all alone.

Is he barking at nothing?

Does he bark at the wall?

Is he talking to someone?

Is it some kind of call?

Does he bark at the moon

and the stars far above?

Is it something he feels?

Is he barking for love?

What goes on in his head
as he barks night and day?

Is there
something important
he's trying to say?

Perhaps it's a language

we can't understand…

Spoken only by dogs

all over the land.

Benny's my best friend,
and he always will be.

But why Benny barks

is a mystery to me.